Summerwood

Summerwood

James Howerton

iUniverse LLC
Bloomington

Summerwood

iUniverse books may be ordered through booksellers or by contacting:

iUniverse LLC
1663 Liberty Drive
Bloomington, IN 47403
www.iuniverse.com
1-800-Authors (1-800-288-4677)

ISBN: 978-1-4917-0529-2 (sc)
ISBN: 978-1-4917-0530-8 (ebk)

Library of Congress Control Number: 2013915433

Printed in the United States of America

iUniverse rev. date: 08/27/2013

This book is dedicated to

Mark Leeker

One . . .

THERE WERE ONLY A FEW safe neighborhoods left in the city, up at Seacrest and Ocean Estates and Green Haven. They were so gated and walled-off that even the cops couldn't get into them. The rest of the city had pretty much collapsed—so goddamn fast—under the weight of people and more people and more people and more people and more people and more people and more people. That was only a quarter of a century ago. Now there was Dream.

Lieutenant Derek Knox told his mind to ignore the city and not remember how it had been back then, when he and Johnny threw the ball at the park. His job did not suffer distractions gladly. Best now to go into robot mode and concentrate on the bounty.

He drove to a gas station and changed clothes. When he emerged he was a slightly ratty denizen with a fake beard and long greasy hair (he had lost his own years ago), and one of the long drab trench coats that were ubiquitous these days, as if everybody had something to hide. He tossed his bag of good clothes into the car and drove down to what used to be the Little Italy neighborhood. It had been a quiet middle-class area, family oriented and kept crime-free by, ironically, the mafia.

But the old goombahs and goodfellows had long ago vanished, and now Little Italy was known as Dream Alley (a misnomer if there ever was one). Cops—the smart ones—stayed away from this place. The dumb ones, like him, did their hunting here because you could record a good week's quota in a couple of days and then scoop up the extra pay from then on. The more danger the more pay. The money for him was where there weren't a lot of questions asked.

He was pretty sure that one day he would die down here, or in a worse place, popped by a laze that some skink carried. It only took one second of carelessness. He needed the extra money to keep Johnny alive at the clinic for as long as possible. And he wondered when his sister Liz would go down the same road, lost in Dream.

Hell of a place to die, he thought, looking at the diseased concrete world. He pulled the car over to a crumbled curb. Little Italy was now a great canyon of abandoned buildings, alleys and dark stinky warrens where god knows what human insects crawled. It had gone down the tubes very quickly, as the whole world had, as if a last fatal weight had dropped on humanity and caused it suddenly to collapse. Many people wandered around Black-Plaguelike, their eyes stunned at the sudden monster. Now it was reversing itself; the world was curing itself, according to fanatics like Allison and the weird Dr. Grey.

Even in Derek Knox's lifetime more people had been born than died. Now millions more died than could ever be born. People, in their despair, most of them, didn't dare have children.

It had happened so fast that society wanted desperate answers. Dream was the number one culprit, widely regarded as the most dangerous and addictive drug in the history of mankind. A demon pill that, in the wake of so many millions of corpses, had to be wiped out. Hence Derek Knox's monthly paycheck.

Social scientists like Allison likened it to what opium did to the Chinese so long ago, only on a global scale. Knox wasn't sure that Dream was to blame for this. It had destroyed his brother's life and was destroying the life of his sister. But he had never tried it, and really knew nothing about it. Addicts never talked about what it did for them. The mantra was that unless you tried it, you could never understand. No, he didn't quite blame the drug for this. It was a long-ignored catastrophe that only needed something like Dream to pull the trigger.

He got out of his car and melted into the dirty and aimless crowds of people who were always wandering this area, going nowhere. He wore dark sunglasses so that he could look around without attracting attention. In this game there was only one mistake, one careless moment.

If they passed the Compassion Act, Johnny's days were numbered. That would free up money at the end of the month that Knox could put away, save for a time when he could escape—he didn't know where—before it was too late. He had always known that it was wasteful keeping a drug addict in a coma—especially in this day and age. But he remembered the old days, and how Johnny had been before the Dream.

Allison had told him that when a Dream addict has crossed the line he falls completely into the story he's created. She didn't truly know; but he suspected that she was right. The rare times Knox had gone to see his brother at the clinic he was shocked at the wasting skeleton in the bed. But Johnny always wore a blissful smile, as if he'd been done up by a very skillful mortician.

Knox kept his brother alive so that Johnny could have his story as long as possible. The Compassion Act would end that, probably for the better. Then it might be possible, in a year or two, to save enough money to get out. Plenty of cops felt the same; that's why they took bribes.

He stopped fantasizing and forced his mind back to business. He had noticed his mind straying lately, like a lost dog trying to find its way home; and that was not good.

Limping down the sidewalk, Knox furtively glanced into the alleys. Finally he spotted a shadow slumped against a wall in the half-darkness.

He limped into the alley, looking as harmless as possible. The skink eyeballed him. This was a dumb one, probably driven off the street and into the alley by the Manx, or a local muscleman.

"Hey, Pa. You need some D?" It came that easy down here in the alleys.

"That's what I'm here for."

"I'll set you up."

"What have you got?"

"I got it all. All the way from 15 minutes to an hour."

"Give me a 15."

Knox didn't want to arouse the skink's suspicions by ordering a full hour; already this guy was wary. He peered at Knox with yellow, bad-liver eyes. "How many times you done it, Pa? I really never seen you before."

"Just twice."

"You a cop?"

"No."

"You gotta tell me if you are."

"I'm not." Knox sighed impatiently. "How much?"

"A blue? One grand."

This was a test. "I got it before for 800," Knox said.

"From who?"

"From Po Boy, down at 57th and Conrad Bridge." Knox was getting sick to his stomach. Everything smelled garbagy and rotten down here. Everywhere. It was a tired stink, like a dying old man who could no longer bathe.

"Po Boy—I knew him," the skink said, studying the greasy wall of the abandoned building. "Po Boy went out there. Too much sampling of the product."

"I could trust him."

"Trust." The skink thought that was amusing. "800, eh? Well, that may've been the 57th price, but here it's a grand."

"That's too much."

"You can't pay too much for a sweet dream. You don't want to spend too much time in this shithole world, you'll go bee-wack. You can go somewhere you're a hero, not a cripple. And you don't want to be prowling around this part of town for long. The Manx are moving in. You don't want one of them catching you."

Knox pretended to shudder—a faked spasm of fear. He knew all about the Manx and where they were going. "We can split the difference. One 15 for nine hundred."

The skink stared away at nothing. In an alley buy you wanted to make them slightly afraid of you, what you'd do if they over-priced.

"I'll be back, probably for a white," Knox said. You'll make money."

"Okay. Nine hundred you get 15 minutes of paradise. You know how long 15 minutes can be in dreamland."

"I know," Knox lied. "Okay, let's get this done. I want to get out of here."

"Don't blame you." The skink fished in a pocket of his filthy overcoat, showing Knox for good measure a laze. It was an expensive one—Grandyear Special, Knox guessed. The skink withdrew and opened a container and, as his eyes blinked up and down from Knox's face to the container, popped out a small blue pill. Okay, here was probable cause, not that that mattered anymore. Him showing the laze was good enough self-defense.

"One more time." The skink just fingered the handle of the laze. "You a cop?"

"No, I'm not a cop."

"Okay, let's see the money, Pa."

Knox reached into his overcoat and drew out his own laze. "No, don't do it. Take your hand off that." Knox aimed the laze at the guy's forehead. "Don't try to run."

The skink stared at Knox's laze. It remained steadily fixed on his forehead, in case the guy was wearing a carbshield vest.

At last the skink found his voice: "Is this a rip?"

"No. I am a cop."

"You said you wasn't."

"I did? I don't remember."

"Hey, what is this, Pa? You can't—"

"I'm not your Pa." Knox fired the laze and the skink's head exploded, spraying brain, blood, skull, cranial mess all over the old brick wall. It was always slushy and ugly, one of the worst moments in a job that had a lot of bad moments. In this close alley the shot was like a flashbulb going off on one of those old black-and-white 20th Century cameras. Knox blinked away fuzz balls. He knelt down and took the laze out of the guy's pants. It was indeed a Grandyear, model 405. Top of the line. Burn a hole through concrete.

He looked down both ends of the alley. Usually it wasn't this easy. Then he removed the container of Dream from the trench coat, opened it and placed it and the laze on the skink's chest. Taking a digital camera out of his trench, he snapped a few pictures from various angles. Then he stood and strode quickly away. At the nearest sewer drain he dumped the pills, red, blue, white into the system that would carry them away with the rest of the filth of the city, into the East River. He would turn the Grandyear into the Evidence, Self-Defense File. He laughed, which was a crazy thing to do.

That's a lot of dreams down the drain, he thought.

Two . . .

AT SUNDOWN THE WHITE TRUCKS rolled out. They resembled modified garbage trucks, only these moved almost silently, their loading mechanism mere whispers of compressed oil.

While the neighborhood slept, the huge white trucks ghosted block to block, the men in white haz-mats scurrying out to examine the figures propped against concrete buildings or sprawled in the gutters. They still had to make sure the individual was truly dead and not just dream-dead, but passage of the Compassion Act would change that. No physician or scientist had ever been able to bring the dream-dead back to life—no drugs or therapies. When the line had been crossed and one last fatal dose taken, you slid into a coma from which there was no return. The figures who had died in the parks and alleys and on sidewalks were quietly loaded into the white trucks and hauled off to the crematoria. If the dead carried i.d.s, the identity would be recorded.

A business of public sanitation and safety. The quiet business of trying to sweep away a ghost world. No one spoke of it when the sleeping figures disappeared. No one ever spoke of the rats.

Derek Knox didn't sleep much these days. Often he would stand at the window of his apartment and stare out at the night and wait for the white trucks to appear. At least some parts of the city were still functioning.

Across the street was the old Newton Street fire station, now an abandoned cave of darkened brick. Otherwise this part of Newton Street was mostly squalid apartment buildings. Some nights he could hear the wind moan under the rusty railroad bridge two blocks away. Quiet had settled over this roaring city, as Dream worked its death spell. It seemed to be falling wearily into sheer silence.

It had happened so goddamn fast, as if the steady poles of reality had instantly reversed themselves.

It had suddenly and impossibly become an upside down world: cops were rewarded for Not bringing in criminals. No longer any jail space or food to feed them, and the wretches who occupied what space there was, who out of desperation to stay alive had turned themselves in, were virtually starved to death. The police department had developed only two cardinal rules. Number One: Never take the law into your own hands. Rule Number Two: Ignore the first rule.

Gustav Arnold, the man who had synthesized Dream 40 years ago, had been executed when he let the formula slip out. From then on, Dream had spread virus-like across the globe. Half the living population called Arnold a monster, half called him the savior of the world. Because, as Dr. Grey explained, Arnold may have provided Earth's last hope for salvation: it killed vast millions of people. And it only killed people.

He'd heard Hugo mutter one drunken night: "It's got rid of the scum and left more for the rest. Might sound cruel; I know they call it a plague. But it's a plague that, you don't want to catch it, don't take the pill. Nobody says it, Deke; but bet your ass and your elbows they all think it."

Under the Green Street railroad bridge he popped two more, a skink and his girlfriend working together. This was turning out to be an easy payday, and he allowed himself just a sliver of hope for the future.

But that was enough. Lately his radar had been tweaking all over the place, and sometimes he found himself shaking like some old bum with the D.T.s. He was fifty years old, and decades of cigarettes and booze had taken their toll. The street was figuring out what cops were doing these days, and they were firing back without warning. How long could a secret like that be kept? Probable Cause, Self Defense; that all washed down at the station, but here on the streets it was really spazzing the dealers out. What truly scared cops (Knox anyway), was not danger, or even violence. It was unpredictability. It was chaos. And he could smell that coming as if it were the creeping stink of mustard gas.

He checked into the office, where Hugo gave him the news: "Ralphie got it last night, down under Madison Bridge."

Knox couldn't talk for a moment. The worms rolled in his stomach. He'd worked Madison Bridge, and it wasn't good. He gave Hugo a look. "Skink?"

"Not sure yet. Could have been one of those Manx bastards. He got it right in the belly, deep under the bridge. He would've laid there til the rats ate him if we hadn't gone looking for him."

"We should go down there and blow away everything that moves."

"A lotta guys are saying just that. It's gonna all come to that anyway."

"Jesus—Ralphie." Knox stared out the office window.

"I know," Hugo said, watching him. "You don't know if you want to go out there, hearing that. Do you?"

"I can't afford not to. I'm damn near broke."

"Well, where's it going to be for you this puke-ass morning?"

"Jones Street." Knox frowned out the window, thinking of Ralphie. His stomach went into half-sick mode. No, he didn't want to go out there. "Gut shot. Why wasn't he wearing his carbs?"

"He was. Bastard used a Stabber. Looked like a Model 103 wound."

Now it was full-sick mode. "How the hell could a skink under a bridge afford that?"

"It was probably a Manx; they got the money."

On his way to Jones Street Knox tried to clear his mind. He had only vaguely known Ralphie; didn't know if the guy had a wife and kids . . .

Around him the dusty wind blew trash down the corridors of half-abandoned buildings. Here and there skeletons lay against the buildings where they had been propped by angry commuters who righteously just wanted them out of the way.

11

He dreaded Jones Street, although it was a lot classier than the downtown alleys. He tried not to think about Stabbers on the streets. All his years in the P.D. he had grown to trust his carbs, as if they were a natural part of his body.

Not now. He knew that he had been doing this too long; that he had the serious gut-worms. They never quit; the gut-worms were always with him now. Knox had gone to a place where he didn't want to live and he didn't want to die; he just wanted the gut-worms to end.

Here on Jones Street some people still occupied the buildings, setting up crude apartments where they could at least exist. These were the people, a majority of the city, who were hunkering down, waiting for the nightmare to be over. Then to emerge into a world stinking of dead, and to maybe start over?

The good people here still looked after one another, but that would change. Knox had skimmed his share of bribes down here, but he had yet to kill a skink anywhere near Jones Street. But all rules change, and they were changing quick. Now there was nothing but the bounty. Now Probable Cause (meaning everything that wasn't Probable Cause), gave Derek Knox a certain grey authority to simply shoot a dealer to death, as long as he had documentation and photographic evidence proving Self Defense. Not such a bad deal, really. He'd been with the department so long they didn't even look at the evidence he turned in. They made sure another Dream dealer was dead, and Knox got his bounty.

Jones Street was lazy this day. Mid-level honest workers, blue collar and white, went about their jobs. The dealers here on Jones were the clever don't-ask skinks. And you couldn't just pop one of them out in the open.

You had to try and lure them out of sight; that was too much trouble. Down here Knox just took the easy bribe. Why didn't it seem so easy anymore?

Not so long ago Jones Street was a cop's candy shop that operated on a pure wink-wink protection model. You get busted, pay the cop—he caught you, bye bye. Knox would rather kill a skink than shake him down, although he knew that was a stupid way to operate. A dead skink didn't show up dealing on the same corner tomorrow.

Now that the Manx were here, it was getting dicey. The Manx were the protection now. And knowing that the police department was bankrupt and could no longer protect their own, they were beginning to use Stabbers to eliminate the competition.

Still, there were plenty of skinks left down here, and the bounty was twice L.I. or East River Bridge or Black Town. You get popped in one of the really gross and sewery areas a bum would at least report it to get the tiny reward. Get popped here on Jones Street and you might disappear forever into a grave littered with ancient plastic bottles and rubbers and empty Dream containers.

Knox was dressed today like a modestly successful businessman. These kind came to Jones Street because there wasn't much violence down here. Still, the gut worms were worse working here, where the strange air of a good community mocked the eyeball truth. He was scared coming here, after all these years never even thinking about it. He parked his car and got out and walked up the three blocks to Jones Street.

Very bad changes were coming, fast. Bad for a cop, anyway.

He saw muscled thugs on street corners and around an open waste that had once been a neighborhood park. They wore the same tattoo on their bulging forearms; the black inverted cross of the Manx. They didn't hide themselves from the law—now they flaunted themselves. They advertised the Manx and its growing power.

In the crowd of shuffling people on the street were probably other undercover cops or DEA, because there was a lot of bribe money down here. The idea gave him some comfort; if you got into trouble they'd help you out—for half the bounty.

He affected a slight limp and kept his head down, just one more human cockroach existing but not particularly alive. However, his eyes were alert, in hunter's mode. Jones Street was trying to put on the face of cool urban comfortable neighborhood, even as it saw Dream spread everywhere. The stink here was different, but still barf-bad. So many people who probably hadn't showered in months. Garbage everywhere that would never get hauled away; and of course the dark smell that had become part of the air: the smell of dead humans.

He scoped the crowds to see if he could spot the signs of a DEA or another cop. It was a million times safer to skim bribes with a partner, even though you had to split the dough.

He wanted to make a quick two or three pops today; then get away. Down here the dealers worked openly on the street. Figuring out that cops were doing executions now, they tended to stay in crowded areas. And they had Watchers covering their backs. Here it was make a deal, then flash the badge and get paid fast as possible. Then you leave this guy alone the rest of the day. Most cops worked this way, because it was infinitely safer than going into one of those alleys.

Knox tried not to work that way. His rage over what had happened to Johnny wouldn't suffer Dream dealers to live.

His attitude, Hugo reminded him, would get him killed.

Like so many cops, Hugo had started out gung ho against Dream. Then he went the predictable route from indifference to fatalism. Knox was sure that, like so many other cops, Hugo was now taking serious bribes from the Manx and other drug cartels. In these days of chaos and panic it was easy to grab what you could before it got worse. And then try to get out.

New thugs were lounging along the street, watching the crowds. They all wore the inverted black cross tattoo on their forearms. The worms moved in his stomach. They weren't wasting any time.

The Manx were named for their founder, Stan Manx, a murderously successful Dream dealer, as evil as they come, but a brilliant organizer and inspirer. Some cop had popped him a couple of years ago, and he became—you guessed it—an instant martyr. The cop who shot him had been literally skinned alive and left hanging from a streetlight.

Knox threaded the crowds that moved down Jones Street. It wasn't long before he spotted a maybe, a raw looking guy who whispered at the crowd passing by. Knox strode past, and—ha ha—the guy took the hook.

"Need some D?" the skink whispered, not looking at him.

"Yes. I'd like a white. I want to do this quickly."

"Quick's my game, Pa. One white, 2K."

15

"All right. I want to do this quickly, okay?"

The skink shrugged. He was a little too indifferent, and Knox's radar tingled. Get this over with. Knox touched his right palm and his badge appeared on his forearm. "P.D.," he said. "Give me the bounty and go on your way. I won't bother you."

The skink looked at him. "I'm Manx," he said. There was craziness in his eyes. That worried Knox.

"I don't give a shit who you are!" Knox spread open his suit coat and showed his laze. "Let's do this and be gone. Give me the bounty. Here on Jones Street—you damn well know—is 3K. So pay me 3K or get yourself arrested for possession of Dream."

The skink looked at him with wondrous amusement. "You a police officer, eh? That's funny. The Manx own this place now. No more Po coming down here trying to strong-arm our people. No more, cop. No more."

To his astonishment the skink pulled a laze right out, here in a scattering crowd, and leveled it at him. Knox pulled his laze. His mouth tasted copper. "Don't make me shoot you!"

"Fuck you, cop."

Knox ducked and fired, but the beam bounced away into space like a light beam striking a mirror. The guy was wearing carb. Oh, shit.

He dove down and rolled away as the skink's laze fired. Knox felt the air blister past his face. He struggled to his feet and sprinted away toward his car. At the extinct park he dodged behind a tree and tried to catch his breath. The Manx thugs had watched, and now they were gathering, all displaying the upside down black cross. He jumped back as a blast struck the tree, showering him with splinters. Oh, God, he thought.

Knox spun out from the tree and started to aim. But the skink had melted into the mess of panicked people on Jones Street. The Manx thugs were surrounding him. He lifted his hands, one holding the pistol, and trotted away from them toward his car.

They didn't fire at him. It was still bad to kill a police officer. This was a warning. As he ran toward his car he could hear them laughing. He looked around and saw them dancing, showing their tattoos.

"Fuckheads," he said. "Jesus friggin God."

"Don't freak out, you pussy!" he yelled to himself as he ran for his life. He dove into his car and started it up. What's wrong with you, Pussy!

He pulled the car over a few blocks from Jones and tried to catch his ragged breath. I thought I was dead. I thought that was it, down on Jones Street. Guy had a Stabber, and he was wearing serious carbs. He thought of Ralphie. God, oh God, this is heart attack shit.

He sat for over five minutes mopping the sweat from his face. Why? Why, Pussy!

Finally he recovered his breath and looked up at a group of children passing the car, staring at him.

What world are you going to get?

He pulled into the liquor store and got a quart of whiskey—two days pay.

He still had the shakes, and it pissed him off. He'd been shot at before—not with a Stabber—but this time got him. He was pretty sure the skink had been ordered not to kill him—this time. Seeing those thugs with the inverted black crosses on their forearms—that's what had really spooked him.

He felt a painful prickle on his neck; splinters from the tree. He sat in his car in the liquor store parking lot and, between sips of the bottle, pulled the tree-splinters out of his arms and tried to calm down. How to escape before the last pillar falls and chaos rules the world. There was no such thing as Retirement anymore. You wanted to quit and walk away, you turned your badge in, your laze, your car, and hit the door.

He wished that he had saved some money over the years, but with the two failed marriages and now Johnny's expenses, that had been impossible. And stupid as it seemed now, he had somehow convinced himself that it would never get this bad.

You fool—it's going to get worse.

Three . . .

HE SAT IN ALLISON'S OFFICE; he didn't look her in the eye.

"You're still shaking," she said.

"I've been drunk for two days."

Allison was an attractive woman in her late thirties. Honey blonde, a jogger. Healthy. Knox always felt like a living corpse around her.

"I can't blame you," she said. "Situations that involve great violence and danger—terror experiences . . ."

"I know I know I know. This one wasn't all that violent; it just shocked the hell out of me that he would take a shot in a crowd of people. I've had worse 'encounters'. And it probably wasn't all that dangerous. It's still a big one to gun down a cop, especially with so many witnesses. I think they just wanted to scare me—and they did. I'm having nightmares about it every night. I don't know why, unless this was the one to finally spill the jar. I think I'm finally getting the Jeebs, Ally." He looked up at her. Allison was studying him with her soft-comfort-hard-analytical face. Something was different in her expression. "What's wrong?"

"They fired me," she said matter-of-factly. "Got my two-weeks notice a week ago. But I knew it was coming a long time ago."

He stared at her with a frown; but why should he be surprised. A bankrupt police department just trying to cope with That out there. How do you justify keeping a police psychologist on the payroll? Allison had probably only kept her job this long because of her family. Knox felt bad for her (God knows he'd miss her), but she came from a rich family, and she lived in Cedar Park, away from this; and she never had known just how bad it was.

"I'll be okay. I've actually developed a sense of relief, a sense of freedom, although God Almighty couldn't find a job for a psychologist out there."

"I'm sorry, Ally."

"I'll be okay. I don't know about you. Why can't you just walk away from it?"

"Can't afford to." Knox picked at his trouser leg, a habit that betrayed his nerves. "I don't want to end up under cardboard; and that'd happen not long after I left this job."

"At least don't go back hunting on Jones Street."

"Don't worry—I won't. The thing is, Allison, they Knew I was a cop the second I got out of my car. It was like they were expecting me. I been out there long enough to smell a real bad wind. Things are changing, and faster than anyone can comprehend. Get out, Ally. Get out of here and don't look back."

"Get out where?"

"Anywhere; just get out of the city."

"You're sounding paranoid, Derek."

"Am I?" He laughed at the window of her office, where her fern sat in the dusty sunlight.

"Put in a transfer out of narcotics."

"I need the bounty money. I still got Johnny to look after, such as he is."

"The Compassion Act will pass," she said.

"I know. It should."

"Do you feel guilt?" She looked away from his eyes. "About what you do? Maybe it's finally rearing its ugly head."

"About what I do? I try to rid the world of drugs that kill people. No, I don't feel guilt."

"I mean the other. It's no secret anymore what you guys do out there. I don't have the right to judge you—"

"About what we Do out there? Like what?"

"Like commit executions."

He shrugged at the fern, the window. "No, I don't feel especially guilty, Doctor."

"You can't blame Dream for all of this. It's no more than a synthetic hallucinogen."

"It seems to be more than that." He looked at her. "You ever try it, Ally?"

"A long time ago, when I was in college," she said. "Twice, that was all. I felt that if I was going to make a career out of treating Dream addicts, I should know what it was all about. You've never tried it, I'm sure."

"Hell no. I don't want to wind up propped against a building starving to death in La-La land. If I get it with a laze, that's a good enough way to go."

"Maybe you should try it," she said. "See what you're fighting, what you want to wipe out."

"That's what my sister keeps telling me: you can never understand unless you go there, into your story, that kind of drool. But she won't tell me much about her trips, where they take her; only that it's sort of religious in nature."

"Every person has a unique story; that's the remarkable property of it."

"And nobody talks about their story; where the stuff took them." He was very tired.

"No." She looked out her office window.

"And you won't tell me where it took you."

"No. It wouldn't do any good to talk about it." She turned and gave him a sardonic smile: "You're probably the only officer on the force who hasn't tried it, at least once."

"Well, I don't know what it does For people; but I sure as hell know what it does To them."

She sighed and gave him a sad, weary smile. "You'd better go say goodbye to Johnny, Derek. Once the bill passes they're going to move very fast on it. They've been preparing for the last eight months."

Four . . .

HE DID GO AND SAY goodbye to Johnny, only a day after the bill was passed. It was like saying goodbye to a wax figure.

It was no good thinking about how things had been when they were kids. Johnny had really died the second he took one last fatal dose and went out there, full into his mind-story.

"Goodbye, Johnny," he heard his voice whisper.

He flinched as a hand came gently down on his shoulder. Dr. Peyton Grey gave him a sad smile. "Well, it's finally all over," he said.

"Yeah, it is."

"When you've said your goodbyes, come back to my office."

"I've said them," Knox said. "Let's go."

Dr. Grey, he knew, had been a loudly vocal advocate of the Compassion Act for some time; even though its passage would put him out of work. It couldn't have been all that easy, keeping dead people alive all those years. People lucky enough (or unlucky enough), to have families willing to pay the increasingly steep price to keep loved-ones alive.

Dr. Grey leaned back in his office chair and gazed away at nothing for a long moment. Knox got himself a cup of coffee and sat down. "How long's Johnny got?"

He liked Doc Grey because the old man never sugared what he said; he was bluntly, brutally honest, and Knox appreciated that.

"Tomorrow that entire ward gets cleared out. By the day after there won't even be beds there; i.v.s will all be gone. There won't be anything left but a huge empty room. Then they'll start tearing down the whole clinic. It was bought up by a consortium. Who knows what they want to put up here. Then your brother will be cremated. You can stop by and pick up his ashes in a few days; I'll call you."

"Don't bother; I don't know what the hell I'd do with them. Sis might want them."

"Liz was in here yesterday, as a matter of fact; not long after the "Act" was made public. She loved her brother."

"Everybody loved Johnny."

"I'll call her after . . ."

"She'll be the next one." Knox scowled.

"You never know." Doc Grey lifted his glasses to his head and rubbed at his eyes. "Lots of folks out there take Dream on a regular basis and never go over the edge. I've seen it all."

"It's funny: that goddamn drug has ruled both our lives; and I hate it and you love it."

"I don't love it. I consider it the last horrifying hope for humanity, but I don't love it, or what it does."

Knox picked at his trouser leg. "Johnny loved the shit out of it. He was always a daydreamer anyway; he never felt he belonged to the real world."

"He'll be free of all this. You and me, we'll have to go on."

"The last hope for humanity, eh? Because it kills people."

"Yes. And the main thing is it kills only people. Have you ever stopped to think that Dream might be God's way of finally cleansing the earth, before it becomes Mars with plastic bottles?"

"No, I've never thought that."

"My doctoral thesis was about human over-population. The more research I did, the more terrified I became. This is a cure that leaves animals alone, and plants, birds and insects; the pure things of the earth it leaves alone. Everything that is truly important to this planet, it leaves alone. It's penicillin for the earth. Old crazy Gustav Arnold may have been an angel sent by God."

"Well, they didn't seem to have any problem executing him."

"Maybe you are too—a sort of minor angel."

"What?"

"By what you do." Doc Grey stared off. "Has it ever occurred to you that what you do for a living is exactly what Dream does?"

"What might that be?"

"You rid the world of humans. You kill those who are deemed unfit to live in this time of madness. I worry about your safety, Derek. But I'm grateful for what you do."

"You're in the tiny minority," Knox said. "I popped two dealers the other day. They were young, a skink and his teen-age girlfriend. They were scared, but I popped them anyway—Self Defense. You're grateful for that?"

"God help me, I am. That kind of population explosion—that's what it was, and I predicted it long ago—could only have one grim cure. Explosion is a good word, because it hit us faster than we could ever have imagined. Now we're going through the great kill; and when it's over the world will have a chance to survive. That's what I believe, God forgive me. What do you believe, Derek?"

"Nothing," he said.

Five . . .

HE WAS RELATIVELY DRUNK WHEN a knock on his apartment door brought him to his feet. It was rare for him to get visitors, as he kept his place terminally unfit for company. Unholstering his laze, he crept to the door and looked out the peephole. It was Liz.

He let her in, and she wrinkled her nose at the sour smell.

"They sell room deodorizers at the dollar store," she remarked.

"I'm never really here that much." He did feel a little embarrassed, throwing dirty clothes off the chair so she could sit down.

"You could pick the place up. You could try," she said.

"I don't see why; there isn't really any point."

"Well, anyway, I just picked up Johnny . . . I thought I'd swing by to see how you're doing."

"You picked up a box of ashes. Johnny's gone."

"Well . . ." Liz was watching him. "I brought you a present. I thought long and hard about it, and I thought it might be the only way to help you." She placed the blue pill on his coffee table.

"No," he said. "Are you crazy, Liz? You could be arrested for having that thing in your purse. I could arrest you."

"You guys are hunting bigger game these days. And I can see what it's doing to you."

"Well, now that Johnny's gone I have a plan. Call it a long term exit strategy."

"Good. I don't want to hear about you under some bridge with half a skull."

"Anyway, that stupid pill isn't going to change anything."

"You might be surprised. I've been reading a book about real dreams, the normal kind you have every night. One theory is that when you dream your mind is taking out the trash, so to speak; clearing it out of your head, all the stresses and fears and insecurities and panic you've accumulated during that day. It does it symbolically through short plays that rarely make sense. It's said that if you didn't dream you'd go insane."

"I don't need a pill to dream," he said. "Believe me, I dream just fine."

"Call it a vacation."

"I can't afford a vacation."

"Yes, you can. Deke, I've never seen anybody who needs one more than you. I don't want to lose both of my brothers."

He laughed. "That's funny; I'm trying to save my kid sister from drugs and she's trying to get me to take drugs."

"Just do it once. It won't kill you, it won't get you hooked. All it'll do is take you away for awhile. From this." She gestured at his apartment window. "And that."

"I used to keep that window open to air the place out," he said. "But then the stink out there got worse than it is in here."

"Just try it," she said. "It's only fifteen minutes out of your life."

"I'm going to flush it down the toilet, so you might as well keep it. You know that this little pill sitting on my coffee table could get me fired."

Liz was studying him. "I don't want to lose you; you're the only family I have left. And you're getting lost, Deke; you're getting lost fast."

He frowned. "It comes with the job. I don't have the luxury of working in a toney coffee shop with all my lesbian friends and dropping Dream every weekend."

"You don't have the right to judge, you bastard." Lizzie's blue eyes always got dark when her Irish went up. "You gave up that 'right' the moment you started going out there and executing people."

"Oh, Christ—you believe that conspiracy crap. Cops are murdering people, that garbage?"

"Yes, I do. You're no longer a cop, you're an executioner. You know it and I know it. So why not just speak the truth."

"Look, if I need psychoanalysis I'll go to Allison. Until then—"

"Allison's not around anymore. Johnny's not around anymore. A hell of a lot of people aren't around anymore."

"That's the way it works."

"Is it?"

29

"That's right. You can't escape by taking some little pill, Liz. That's only going to take you down the same road it took Johnny. And when your pretty dream is over you still gotta deal with that out there, past that window."

She stood and picked up her purse. "Try it, Deke. Believe me, you need it."

"You over dose on that shit," he said. "I won't be able to keep you alive. They'll just give you a shot to stop your heart; then it's off to the ovens."

She walked to the door. "You should at least know what you're killing people for."

"That pill's going into the toilet a minute after you're gone. Believe me, Sis, I've disposed of more Dream than you could imagine."

"Try it," she said.

When Liz was gone he sat staring out the window. Then he looked at the blue pill.

"I know where you're going, you little bastard." Scooping up the pill he marched back to the bathroom. But he didn't flush it. Looking around his filthy, stinky apartment he felt a crushing despair. Did anything matter anymore? Or were people just pretending, and waiting for a better time when things would start to matter again. My place stinks. No room deodorizer is going to do any good. Everything around me stinks; everything out there stinks!

Okay. I've popped a lot of skinks on your behalf, he said to the pill. I suppose I finally owe it to you to finally pop you and find out who you really are. Fuck it. Fuck every stinking thing.

He prepared himself. He pulled the curtains, shut off his cellphone and, without any more consideration, drew a glass of tap water and swallowed the blue pill. He lay down in bed and closed his eyes and waited.

There was nothing for about a minute; then his brain began to go into an oozy unreality. He wasn't scared; he felt very calm, as a matter of fact. Well, I did it, he thought. I crossed the line, and I no longer have the right to call myself a legitimate cop. You fool, you were never a legitimate cop. That species went extinct long ago . . . Sis was right: you're an executioner.

He came awake and stared up at dappled sunlight. His first sensation was a feeling of physical freshness, as if he had awakened from a deep, restful sleep. He sat up on soft grass and gazed around: he was in a glade, and he could hear a stream in the distance. A primitive path wound down into the glade from a dense elfin forest. The air was clean and lush. Wildflowers grew on either side of the path. Not anything he had expected.

He was dressed like Robin Hood, and he wondered if he Was. He only knew vaguely the tales of Robin Hood, so he kind of doubted it. But sure enough, next to him in the grass lay a bow, and next to that a quiver of arrows.

Well, this is crazy enough, he thought. I've never fired a bow and arrow in my life. And I never had a fixation on knights or that medieval forest shit.

His pants were of some soft calfskin or other. His white shirt was linen, he guessed. Leather boots touched his knees. His jacket was brown, and a brown cape and hood flowed over him in the breeze. The clothes felt very comfortable, as if he were back home in his sweats.

Back home. He smiled. You're still home, dumb ass. You're still laying on your smelly bed a stupid cop with no future but a splashed head under some filthy rusting bridge. This is a goofy drug trip.

He stood and absorbed the scenery. Through the giant trees he could see the stream, winding silver around boulders. Most of the trees were oaks, he guessed; though smaller trees clothed the stream (willows?).

It was a magic world; he had to give his imagination credit for that. He felt exhilarated staring at this—even knowing it wasn't real. He had had dreams (only a few of them), that were so poignant and sweet and perfect that he had not wanted to wake up to the sore work of life. For the first time he understood the blank-eyed people propped up against the buildings, soft smiles on their dying faces. Maybe skeletons grin because they really are in a better place.

He stood, feeling surprisingly strong and healthy. He had never felt so good. He took in the beauty of this place, a sylvan landscape that had probably not been seen on Earth in centuries. Sweeping the forest with his eyes, he caught sight of a small group of deer, who watched him with blinking, wary eyes. Reddish squirrels wriggled up the ancient massive trees.

Only they weren't ancient. He had created them not two minutes ago, when he took the pill.

Of course there weren't even minutes here. Dream made its own time, Liz always said.

He stared up the path. It was a mere hard-dirt scar in the green meadow that went up, curved, and disappeared into the shadows of the forest. He wondered where it led, where his tired, ugly brain might take him. So this is what it's all about, he thought, watching woodland birds swoop and flicker into the trees, where dusty beams of sunlight angled down. Pure peace.

This forest around him was alive with chirps and flutters and the scratching scuttling of small, busy animals. Wind whispered to the trees. Even so, he had never felt such *quiet* before. He might as well go up that trail and play in the dream ...

But for a moment his senses were bewitched, and he stood in the Middle Age costume staring around at this primeval world. Apparently his mind, scared and tormented, had conjured up a peaceful paradise, so unlike the grey city, in order to get some rest.

But he didn't want to rest. A wild energy was flowing through him. He felt absurdly fit and strong. Athletic even. He started up the path then remembered the bow and arrows. What the hell, he thought. He took up the bow and strapped the quiver of arrows onto his back, feeling vaguely foolish. There may be imaginary bears in them imaginary woods. He chuckled.

But then a noise came out of the forest, whispering to him to hush up and hide. A faint rumble like distant thunder, only it grew gradually louder. Suddenly a regiment of horsemen appeared around a curve in the woods and rode down into the glade. He stood watching them in wonder. Finally some action in this dream.

They were dressed all alike (soldiers, maybe), in scarlet trousers and black knee boots; light chain-mail vests over black shirts. They wore silver helmets that glinted in the sunlight. They rode up to him and about 10 men dismounted and immediately surrounded him, staring in curiosity. Knox felt like he was in an old Technicolor movie. He gave these men a 360 degree smile, a bit embarrassed that his Dream story might turn out melodramatic and cheesy.

They were tall, swarthy men; and they stared at him in a kind of hostile wonder. Their swords looked real enough.

Then he spied her in the midst of the mounted soldiers. A beautiful woman dressed in a green riding outfit complete with velvet hooded cape. Her hair was in a long severe auburn braid. She was on a pure white horse, gilded with jewels. She watched him with intense, narrow eyes. He couldn't take his eyes off her, which was a mistake because one of the dismounted soldiers had sneaked up behind him and was raising a wooden staff.

"What!" Knox half turned when the staff came whooshing and slammed into the back of his head.

"Spy!" the soldier hissed.

A blinding pain; and as he collapsed to the ground. Knox thought, time to wake up! Time to wake up! This is a bad trip.

"Ahhh! Get this over . . ."

But it wasn't over. He came to and, despite the throbbing knot on the back of his skull, he was too astounded to care, because standing over him was the beautiful girl he had seen in the forest with the soldiers. For his part, he was chained to the floor of a dungeon of some sort.

The girl—young woman—was studying him with some hostility, and he managed a smile. What weirdness a drug can unleash in a tired mind.

"Do you speak English?" he asked.

His voice startled her, but she soon recovered. "I speak your language," she replied after a pause. "Though your speech is strange."

"Right now everything is strange."

"Are you working for the Garmen?" she demanded.

"The Garmen?" He was still squinting up at her, trying to get his brains back. He had never been an especially creative type, and he was surprised that his mind could make such a lovely woman. There was sadness in her face; her eyes seemed to hold a weary tragedy. Maybe she was a composite of all the fantasy girls he had never known. "What are the Garmen?"

She studied his face for deception. "Those who are coming to destroy us."

Chains jingling, he felt the knot on the back of his head, and flinched at a surprising stab of pain. He looked around him: stone walls and shadows; a window of iron bars through which striped sunlight glowed. For a dungeon, the place smelled strangely fragrant—sort of barnlike.

He looked back at her, a ghostly-beautiful image. She had changed her green forest outfit and now wore a long white gown that flowed around her and shimmered like a waterfall. Her long auburn hair fell down her back unbraided. She wore a dainty crown of silver decorated with red and blue gems. "How long was I—asleep?"

"Long enough to bring you here to the castle. My men wanted to hang you straightforth in the forest."

"That would probably have sent me back home. Why do these Garmen want to destroy you?" he played along.

"We stand in their way."

He was amazed at how sad and beautiful her eyes were; he had never seen eyes like hers before. So how could his mind conjure them?

"If you are not in league with them . . ."

"I'm not," he assured her.

"If you are not a spy—then who are you? You do not dress like a Garman."

"I'm a man in a dream, just passing through."

He pulled gently at the chains that held him to the floor. He knew they weren't real; so why couldn't he just will them off?

"The Garmen aren't real." He wondered why he didn't seem to have full control over this. Or any control at all. "Nothing in this story is real. You're not real."

She was studying cautiously for signs of madness.

"This is all a drug I'm on," he tried to explain. "I made this world up—my mind did."

"You claim to be a wizard?"

"Yes. Well, no. More like a sort of god, an imaginary one. In reality I'm a lieutenant on an NYPD narcotics squad. Addicts who pop a pill called Dream will never tell you about where it took them. After a few years it got the best of me and I dropped a low dose of the drug just to see . . . why am I telling you this?"

"If you are a god," she questioned. "Why then did you not stop my soldier from striking you?"

"Good question. I don't know. This is my first trip." He jangled the chains. "Obviously I can't make these go away."

"No, you cannot."

He couldn't help but smile at her. She had such a serious face. It was only a fifteen minute dose; this foolish Olde English Dream would be over soon enough, might as well enjoy it.

"You're quite beautiful," he said to her.

A hint of a blush. Her lips were very full, but the edges of her mouth were naturally sad.

"I am the Princess of Summerwood," she said arrogantly. "No stranger speaks to me that way."

"I apologize, Your Majesty."

Princess of Summerwood? Well, he had never been all that creative.

The breeze blowing in through the barred window was soft and sweet. Flower fragrance and the smell of forest. How long had it been since he'd smelled trees and grass? Had he ever smelled them? Had he ever been any part of the earth?

"Why didn't you let them hang me out there, Princess?"

"My father may want to question you."

"Your father. That would be the king."

"Yes."

"All right. I suppose that'd at least get me out of these. I always wondered that if I ever did break down and take Dream, where the stuff would take me. I never expected something like this."

"Your bow and arrows are of very high quality," she said. Her voice was almost a whisper, but only in its softness. "From what land do you come?"

"America. New York City, to be precise."

"I have never heard of such a land," she said doubtfully. "Just so you know: you were spared death in the forest, but the knights want to execute you as a Garman spy."

"Well, I'm not worried about that. Much as I enjoy your company, I'll be gone soon enough."

"How?"

"When the Dream drug wears off. I only took a small dose. I'm not sure exactly when it will happen. Under the influence of Dream it's said that time isn't the same as . . .

well, anyway, they call it 'dreality', not that you know what I'm talking about."

She studied him in an adorably serious way, still wondering about his sanity. Her simple Maid Marian dress covered a figure that was lithe and athletic. Small breasts; that did not seem to be what his mind would conjure for his personal story; however . . .

"Is this England?" he asked.

She blinked her eyes questioningly. "This is the Kingdom of Summerwood."

"Yes, so you said. Can I get these chains off? I assure you I'm harmless. And I don't want to spend my trip chained down in a dungeon."

He smiled at her, but she didn't smile back. She seemed incapable of smiling. As he gazed into her eyes and smelled the soft fragrant breeze blowing into the dungeon, he felt an overwhelming sense of longing. Of desperately wanting. She was the most fascinating vision he had ever imagined, and he was proud of the creative side of his brain. You sure did it this time, Pal. This is truly not what I thought it'd be. What did Gustav Arnold see when he tried out his new drug on himself. Some strange false heaven?

"I will order them removed," she said at last. "Then you must go and speak to my father."

"The king. King who?"

"King Xellos; ruler of Summerwood."

"What's your name?"

She hesitated. Then, "My name is Cassiel. Your name?"

"Derek Knox." He chuckled, telling his name to a dream. "I can't wait to see your palace and more of this countryside—before I vanish back to reality. It very much sucks compared to this."

"It may be, Dereknox," she said, now showing just a hint of a smile. "That you will vanish before you see it."

Knox frowned as she abruptly turned and left the dungeon, leaving him in sudden quiet. That was disturbing. This was not what he had expected when he dropped the blue pill. To be hanged in the woods or be-headed in a dungeon did not seem to him such a good dream.

But he smelled the sweetness of the breeze, the odor of the straw he lay on. He felt a sadness not like the usual, and he understood at last why addicts would choose to live in their dream world, propped up against the bricks or sprawled out on the sidewalk; normal, disgusted people stepping over them on their way to work and decent lives. He got it all right. He suddenly and powerfully didn't want to leave here, this place. The only thing that he wanted was to stay here and be with her. There was nothing else.

As he waited to be unchained—as he yearned to see Cassiel, again—the air around him began to quiver, this world seen through heat ribbons. He felt himself swept suddenly away into a terrible darkness, and his heart pounded too hard in his chest.

He jumped awake and stared up at the stained ceiling of his apartment. He smelled the stinky must-rot air. He heard cars outside, sirens, the under-roar of the city.

"I'm back," he whispered to the ceiling. It took him two full minutes to get the other world out of his mind. Summerwood, an oak-rich fantasy come to life; and, of course, Cassiel and her tragic face. It's a dangerous thing, Allison had said, trying to hold onto the story.

I'm not going to. I tried it, okay. And it was weird, that's all.

He got off the bed and went to the window, pulling apart the curtains, revealing the grey, ruined city, the bony creatures now being bagged up in the daylight like abandoned mannequins. If they were still alive, it was only the stab of a needle. The government was moving fast on this. They had been prepared to go into action the second the Compassion Act went through. Garbage men ridding the world of dead and dying human beings, and no longer bothering to do it by the dark of night. It was different, though. It was necessary. The stench of death had become one with the air. The familiar weary remains of human civilization shuffled toward nothing.

I'm back, he thought.

Six . . .

"So you tried it!" Liz grinned at him. "Finally my dysfunctional big brother has some fun and adventure."

"It wasn't fun," he lied. "I had to know what the big deal was—and that's the end of it."

"Is it?" Liz gave him one of her lop-sided smiles. "You won't talk about it."

"No, I'd rather not. Liz, this shit is so dangerous that . . . god damn it, Liz, this shit will kill you. I've seen it too many times."

"Finally you've seen something else." She was staring at him with her big wonder eyes. "I see already how it's changed you."

"Don't do any more of that shit—please, for me. Don't do any more. If you wind up like Johnny did, It'd break me, Sis. I couldn't take it."

She took his hands in hers. "You're finally seeing what you've been yearning to see all your life. I was the baby, I never knew the world that you and Johnny had,

41

baseball and all that. What it was—Derek, I can only know with Dream. A world where people go to church every Sunday; where they love and care for one another; a world of green hills and pastures and woodlands and joyous work. I feel alive there, and I feel dead here. I can't say anymore."

"Mine took me to some crazy old English forest, with a fairy princess and all that."

She smiled. "That doesn't seem anything like you."

"I know." He shrugged.

"But then you were always attracted to danger."

"I guess."

"What are you going to do now? Now that Johnny's gone."

"Try to save up enough money to get out of here," he said. "You need to come with me."

"No. I need to stay here."

"Sis, this is getting bad. In your great dream world it might be perfect; but here in reality it's going bad fast; I need to get as much bounty as I can, and you need to save up all you can—and then before it really goes down, we can get out of here with cash."

"I don't want to get out of here, Deke. I want to stay here—because I've been out of here for a long time. Get out of here, if that's what you have to do. But there won't be any places to escape to. You want desperately to hold onto this evil world—but I don't. I want to let it go. I want to give it to the ones who survive."

"You want to commit suicide."

"I want the real world."

"This Is the God Damn Real World!"

"No, it isn't," she said.

"Yeah. That's the drug talking." He stared at the window.

She said nothing. Knox felt despair as never before, one that actually doubled him up. When Mom died of a heart attack and Dad died of cancer he'd promised to look after Johnny and Liz. Now it was all—God, my little sister, who I promised to protect . . . my little sister!

"No!" she said, when he started to speak. "I don't want to commit suicide. But I won't give up Dream. It's the only thing that means anything to me. That's just the truth, Big Brother."

"Dreality—that's what you want? Dreality. It's just another word for suicide."

"You think about her—don't you?" Liz said.

"What?"

"The girl. I know you met a girl. I'll bet she was in danger."

"It was a made-up fantasy, Lizzie—that's all. And as I recall, I was the one in danger. Your little church in the dale—a movie you saw, and now it's over. It doesn't do any good to talk about it. I don't want to talk about it."

"I'm going where I have to go. This life isn't so bad for me. I look down at the pavement whenever I go somewhere; I avoid the monsters as best I can. I make it to work and I feel safe there. Even though just across the street the monsters gather, like hungry baboons, showing everybody their upside down crosses."

"They like to do that," Knox said. "We call them just that, baboons. Only that's unfair to real baboons."

Liz let out a short laugh. "But you have to go down into it. That's your job, to go down into that and deal with that. Deeper and deeper."

"The deeper you go, the more money you make," he said.

"This isn't about money—this is about your life. How long can you keep this up? I talked to Allison, I know what you do!"

"I do my job. And the minute I stop doing my job, I'm out there sleeping under cardboard. You know a lot about dreality, Lizzie—but you don't know shit about reality."

"Maybe not," she said. "I know that it's more than all about money. You think money is going to cure everything."

"It's all about money. You get half your head cut off, and somehow you manage to stumble into an emergency room at one of the hospitals. The first thing they ask you is, 'do you have insurance?' Yeah, Liz, it's all about money."

"Just money?"

He gave her a grim stare. "You can't escape without money."

She grunted. "That changed a long time ago."

"So why are there so God damn many dealers out there trying to scam my money?"

"The addicts are scamming the dealers," Liz said. "Very soon they'll just be walking around with pretty paper in their pockets. They're selling good dreams for useless ones."

He stared out the dirty window: "You won't talk about your story. Why is that? So you can turn your face away from what's real?"

"Nobody talks about their stories. Maybe it's fear of losing them, I don't know."

"Nobody talks about the corpses that are really out there."

"Don't say anymore, Deke."

"The ones that disappear every night, and get replaced."

"Stop it, Derek."

"And the little black scuttlers that leave chunks torn out of the dreamers, not that they'd know. Even the good Doc Grey won't dare talk about that. No, it's all a wonderful perfect dream. Why doesn't anybody talk about the maggots and lice and scuttlers?"

"Shut up!"

Nobody ever talked about the rats, although they were probably the best indication of the future. They came out mostly at night, but Knox had seen bolder ones in broad daylight, perched on the dream-dead. When he hunted at night, Knox would sometimes drive slow down the dark street, and shoot his spotlight over the sidewalks and alleys to see them scurry from the light, some standing arrogantly on their haunches and peering right into the spotlight, their red eyes glowing out of the shadows.

People didn't talk about what happened to a dream-dead who'd been out too long; some smiley skeleton who'd long ago lost everything to Dream; his job his house his car his money his family. To crawl under one of the bridges where they wouldn't find him, or some dark crevice in the city. Cops, when they found them, would vomit at the sight. Knox had, plenty of times. Rat banquets they called them.

Most tried to find a safe mattress somewhere; four walls at least against the streets and the weather, the insects and rats. But there were few places hungry bugs and rats couldn't find. Johnny had been one of the lucky ones. Knox could at least have that. Liz was in a group that looked after one another when one slipped into the coma. They had prepared places where you could finish out your story in peace. Maybe it was right for her to think about her story, in some glittering meadow of God. To think of the saintly figure she had made fall in love with her. And not to think about the rats.

Seven . . .

He met the DEA guy, Eddie, downtown in unlikely Central Park. The guy came up to him, so he was obviously being cased. He sat down heavily on a bench and the DEA joined him.

"Hell of a world," the guy said.

"Yeah, it is."

"When a cop has to be a bounty hunter."

Knox looked at him. He was a stringy guy, a lot meaner and stronger than he looked. DEA had become a wolf pack in the last ten years, and they weren't to be fucked with.

"I'm not a bounty hunter."

"You are, Knox. We all are. And now is the time to get together on this."

"On what?"

"Stop that. We partner up, work the easy bribes, we can bring in six gees a day. Fifty-fifty split, you and me."

Knox laughed. "Is this some kind of sting? You wearing a mic?"

"Those days are over. I've watched you operate, how you spin. You've gotten spooked, and you got the worms—but you and me, working together, could skim enough money to set us up."

"And then what?"

"Then we get out. You want to escape, I want to escape—we work together to escape."

Knox stared off. "What about the Manx?"

"They are what they are. It ain't going to be safe. But it'll be safer if the two of us work together. I've got people in DEA, they know what we're up to, and they encourage it. You been out here long enough, you know what I'm saying."

"Yeah, I know. So we partner up on this, split the bounties."

"They may go up to ten thousand a day, if we work our asses off. The bottom line is, you need the money, Knox, and I need the money. We don't just want the money—we need it."

"Yeah. So what really are you telling me?"

"I got it worked out pretty good," Eddie said. "We start out south, at Pallisades—"

"Whoa," Knox said. "That's not my place. It belongs to the South P.D. They'd sniff me out and sand me down."

"No. Dee trumps the locals. There's a lot of Dees down there. My friends."

"Too much competition for me," Knox said. "I don't know the cops working Pallisades. I know they won't want some up-towner moving in."

"Well, that's the deal," Eddie said. "We partner up, I think we'll make a lot of money."

Knox stared across Central Park. "Why haven't you teamed up with another Dee? You guys sleep together."

Eddie laughed. "Dees are too greedy. It works better with a local cop. You ain't afraid to go into the pits. Maybe you want to. But it's time you applied your skills in a less dangerous and more lucrative way, if you ever want to get out of this place."

"Sell out to the Dream dealers," he said.

Eddie looked him in the eyes. "You didn't know it, but I saw you pop those two kids down under the bridge."

Knox felt the worms moving. "Why didn't you turn me in?"

"No point in doing that. You're a bottom feeder; you're making good money, and you're getting rid of Dream dealers. But you're not one step closer to getting out of here. And back at your department, they're taking bets on when you get popped."

"I like working alone."

"No you don't—that's stupid. I haven't had to pop a skink in over a year. I don't even have to yank dealers in, that's all in the past. You've been out there. Hell, you Live out there. You know; that's why I'm talking to you. So stop thinking about killing the skinks, start thinking about getting their money."

Knox stared across Central Park. This wasn't a sting, he thought. Just last week the department had 'let go' the entire Internal Investigation Division. Don't tell, don't ask. This could be his last way out.

"Why me?"

"Like I said, I been watching you. Main thing about you, Knox, is you're getting desperate."

"I don't have any choice."

"Yeah. Well, that's the deal. Where we'll be working nobody's going to make you. Lotta cops and Dees down there, because that's where the rich kids deal. There's plenty of dough for everybody."

"Not when the Manx move in."

"The Manx get paid to stay away from the south sides. For now, there's good dough to be made; but we gotta make it now, before the shit really hits the fan. Bust ass, score big and get out while we can. Are you blind?"

"I don't know," Knox said.

They worked Pallisades for two weeks and Knox scooped up more than ten thousand dollars. Here it was stroll the sand, get a stupid kid to offer you Dream, then flash the badge and grab three thousand dollars cash. The kids kept a wadded up rubber-banded three k's, figuring that one time they'd get busted. Down here it was just the price of doing business. A few U.C. cops had come up to him and told him to get the fuck back home, but that wasn't going to happen. He'd been where those soft cops would never go.

He lay on the warm beach, his pockets bulging with money, his mind thinking of where he would escape to.

"You ever try that shit?" he asked Eddie.

"Couple of times."

"I tried it once."

Eddie lay out in the sun and smiled. "Pretty intense, eh?'

"Yeah."

"Well don't do it again." Eddie gave him a look. "Now we go to Collier Park."

"Who deals drugs on Collier Park?"

"You'll be really, really surprised."

"I suppose the shit's everywhere," Knox said.

"Now you know why."

"What's that supposed to mean?"

"I knew guys—and women too—had everything going. Money, good safe home, good food. They threw it all away. A good good life and everything you ever wanted. And then they took Dream over and over and over until it pushed them off the cliff and they fell into it."

"That's all it is. Dying the way you pick to die."

"I don't want a partner thinking about his Story." Eddie cuffed him on the shoulder. "I know how it is. But now we need to start skimming Collier Park."

"I'm okay," Knox said.

"You okay, then why'd you snag that white from the kid?"

"What?"

"You snagged a white from that last kid we got. I saw you do it. God damn it, you ain't dealing on the side?"

"No. I wouldn't be much of a dealer with one white."

"I know." Eddie looked away. "You shouldn't do it. Look how good this world is going for us. You went there, okay. But don't go back there. We can make a lot of fast money; but not if you go slipping off into Dream. Don't go back there."

The world was starting to show some hope. No Manx down here; it was just a part in a play, and then payday. No dent in the Dream traffic. That'd be like trying to catch the wind. Much smarter taking the money and not blowing heads off.

"Okay," he said. "Collier Park."

"You be the weird college professor who wants a white."

"College professor?"

"A lot of them live over there. And they got a lot of cash."

They got into Eddie's car and drove onto the freeway, east toward Collier Park. The white pill was in Knox's pocket, but Eddie didn't mention it again. Collier Park was ivy-grown and intellectual. People with money that no one knew how they had acquired. Artists (what there were left of them), writers who wrote of the dark times and the darker times to come. Musicians who sent melodies out the windows into nothing.

"This isn't what I'd call a good hunting ground," Knox said as Eddie pulled up to the wrought iron community gate. "How are we even going to get in here?"

"I've got the security code." Eddie smiled, touched a button on his dash, and the gates crawled opened. "A lot of money here—and a lot of Dream. They pay good dough here to keep things safe; to keep the nightmare away. They just want Dream, that's all. And we just want money. There don't have to be any violence. We can make fifteen thousand here, if we use our skills and do our thing. You cop a bribe, I watch you; I cop a bribe and you watch me. Okay?"

"Okay. I'll give it a try."

He was very good at it. Collier Park was a secret glen of deer, and they were the lions that had sniffed it out. Get some kid to offer you Dream, show your badge and scoop three grand. Half to go to Eddie. A sixty second transaction if you talked fast and looked business. Then you sit and watch, and Eddie gets a skink and flips DEA, and there's another one point five.

Knox slid out the brick in his apartment wall and stuffed the cash in there. He was putting away a lot of money, and soon he would be able to escape. He took the white pill out of his pants pocket. He looked at it. He wanted to go back there—he felt he deserved to go back there. After all the money he'd made, the sleep he'd lost. It was called 'the craving', according to Allison.

This world was falling down around itself. Yesterday the analyst on t.v. had said that even cash was becoming almost worthless, that people were paying anything to the survival warehouses that had sprung up, offering preserved foods, bottled water, even medications for the looming collapse of civilization. Maybe he had waited too long, and it was too late.

He looked at the white pill. He thought of Cassiel. He thought of that woodland realm where he had felt at last alive. Eddie had warned him, and he knew that Eddie was right. But that didn't seem to matter anymore.

He shut off his cell phone and pulled the curtains. He took the white and lay down in his smelly bed and waited. Soon enough the earth swirled around him and he was in Summerwood.

He stared up at a kindly face; an old man dressed as a king. The man studied him, and Knox smiled back, going into this world. Why not?

"I'm back here," he said to the king.

King Xerros studied him. "We never thought you'd wake up. My daughter tells me that you claim to be a wizard."

Knox looked over and saw her standing there, watching them. She was dressed in the silvery gown. Her eyes were very watchful.

"No. I'm only a man passing through."

"Passing through? What does that mean?"

Knox was on a very comfortable bed. He sat up. He felt rejuvenated, he felt strong beyond his body. He had never felt so strong and vital. "I can't tell you what this is all about. Only that it's not real."

"My daughter told me that you said she was not real. What does this mean?"

"It means—I don't care what it means." He looked over at Cassiel, standing in the sunlight. "This is a world my mind created. This is a drug called Dream. Nothing here is real."

The old king frowned. "Do you think you know what is real? Come here, let me show you real."

Knox got off the bed and followed the king to a stone window that let in a faint smoky breeze. Knox looked out. Beyond the gardens and green pastures, beyond the green forests, was a haze of smoke.

"That is the smoke of burning villages. Look down there at my people, fleeing, coming desperately into this palace. The Garmen are burning my kingdom, my people."

"I created the Garmen," he heard himself say. "Maybe I can stop them."

"How?"

"Because none of this is real."

"Why do keep saying that?" Cassiel cried.

"Summerwood is real. The Garmen want to destroy us because we are real." The king looked away, perplexed. "I have no more time for a mad man. My daughter seems to believe that you Are a wizard, and you can help us defeat the Garmen. I believe you to be nothing more than a mad man, unable to give us any aid."

Knox's cop-mode took over: "What kind of weapons do they have?"

Cassiel joined them, sitting down, her silver dress shimmering. She gave Knox a very angry look. "What we have, only more. Bows and arrows, spears, machines that launch boulders at our walls."

"What do you have?"

"We have the same," King Xerros said. "But the Garmen are very strong and very fierce. They are evil, and proud to be evil."

"The Manx," Knox said.

"What?"

"I think I might have created these Garmen in the model of the Manx—real marauders in the real world. My mind is creating what I'm afraid of."

"The people want to execute you as a sorcerer," Cassiel spoke up. "A stranger just appearing in our kingdom, when all this is happening. It was only the word of my father that saved you."

"I have only one thing: to save my people from destruction." King Xerros stared at him. "Be you wizard or not; will you help me?"

"I will," Knox said. He smiled at Cassiel.

"First we want to see how you use your bow," Cassiel said.

"Hmmm. I hope I don't make a great fool of myself."

Surrounded by soldiers, he was led down into a lovely garden just below the palace window. A target was set up too far away to ever hit. He was given back his bow, and he wondered if he would even be able to load it. He had watched old movies and ancient t.v. shows with Indians and the like shooting arrows, so he had a rudimentary idea of how it was done. Too bad he couldn't have brought his laze here, or a few anhydrous grenades.

It was a cool overcast morning, sweet with flowers. Dew glittered in the trees. The sky looked like rain. He saw wretched peasants shuffling quickly in through a doorway of massive oak; archers lined the tall battlements all around the castle; for all the beauty and wonder, there was an unmistakable air of panic.

The king handed him an arrow. The soldiers had their grim eyes on him. Cassiel watched him with her tragic eyes.

"That target is a long way off," he said.

"If you can kill but one Garman you will be of use to me."

Knox fitted the arrow onto the bow string. A strange sense of skill came to him, as if he'd done this a thousand times. Somehow he knew exactly what to do. He felt power in his arms; his eyes saw with clarity everything in this world. He raised the bow and the target seemed almost in his very face. Without a second thought he released the arrow and it shot across the garden and stabbed the very center of the target.

The soldiers began growling at one another. The king handed him another arrow. "They think you are a wizard. Perhaps you are. I have never seen such a shot."

Knox feathered the second arrow and sent it straight, so that it brushed the first arrow aside to find the center of the target. Cassiel was staring at him.

"I could get used to this," Knox said, grinning at her.

"There is little time," King Xerros said. "The Garmen will be at the gates in only two days. If you fight with us, Dereknox, you will be allowed to live. You can kill a target—can you kill men?"

"I've killed many men. Not with a bow."

The king stared away and sighed. His careworn face betrayed great sadness. "The times are evil. We could not be allowed to live in peace; to work our lands and raise our children and make the world a better place. We must always prepare for war. War and War and more War. It never ends. When the Garmen approach, I ask that you station yourself on one of the ramparts. I now leave you with my daughter, for I have to prepare for this terrible thing."

With that, King Xerros turned and marched away. Knox took in the dull, overcast skies, the wet wind that swirled in the trees. He looked at Cassiel. "This is a beautiful kingdom, Summerwood." Knox put down his bow and strode over to a glistening pond. Frogs jumped into the water at his approach. Purple and white lilies floated on the crystal water. He bent down and looked into the water.

"Holy god!" He drew back and caught his breath.

"What is wrong, Dereknox?" Cassiel joined him at the pond.

"The—the reflection. My reflection. I'm in my fifties, I'm bald! That's not me!"

"I do not understand," Cassiel said. "You could not be so old."

Cautiously, Knox looked back into the water. He touched his face. What looked back at him in the sheen of the pond was not him; it was a young handsome man, square-chinned, dashing. Why should it surprise him? Allison had said that some dreams epitomize the ideal. In other words they let you see what you want to see, and be what you want to be. I don't want to be who I am, he thought. So my brain is giving me who I want to be.

Who is that?

"Dereknox." Her voice broke him out of his shock. "Why are you frightened at once?"

"I—I'm not frightened. A little stunned."

"It is only a pond. A place for frogs and flowers and hummingbirds."

"Hummingbirds." He smiled gazing into the glass water. "Tell me; am I what a princess like yourself would consider handsome?"

"Yes, very. But these are not times of love, they are times of war. I know not how or why you came to us. I only know that in two days time the Garmen will be here. Many will die. All we have worked for and cherished will burn. I believe you came here for a reason, Dereknox."

He took her hands, and a soft smile came to her face.

"My God, you Can smile. And what a beautiful smile it is."

"There is nothing to smile about."

He gazed down in the pond at his new face; he felt his new body. He felt Cassiel close to him, her silver gown just touching him in the wind as they sat together on the flat stones that bordered the pond. Green frogs popped their heads out of the water to stare at them. Bright birds fluttered down to drink. Lightning flickered away, where storm clouds were starting to build.

"Then why are you smiling?"

"Because somehow—I do not know how—you have brought hope here."

Eight . . .

"Look at the bod on that one!" Eddie said. "That's pure California fruit. The end of the world and they're out there in their bikinis."

Knox was scoping the beach for game. It was easy here. "That guy there," he said. "The blondie with the long hair."

"Good call. Go on down and meet him."

Knox went down on the beach. He was Jack Normal, in shorts and a tee shirt and wearing a wide straw hat. The blond kid smiled at him, and it was that fast: "You want some Dee?"

"Yeah, a white."

"You a cop? Or DEA? Or FBI?"

"No, I'm not. I just want to get a white, that's all."

The kid pulled out a packet of whites, and Knox showed his badge. "P.D.," he said. "No, stay still. I only want the take, and then I'll be on my way, and you won't have to worry about me rest of the day. All right?"

"How much?" the kid said.

"You know how much, Prick! Three Gees and your stash. Trust me, it's better than jail."

"I don't have three gees. Here, I can give you my stash."

"And three gees. You're not stupid enough to deal down here without a payoff."

Knox looked up at Eddie, standing watch on the pier. All at once Eddie made a frantic gesture. The blonde kid bolted and was running away down the sand beach. Knox pulled out his laze and put the red dot on the kid's head.

"Stop! Police! Stop where you are!"

He heard Eddie yell out, "No! Let him get away!"

But the scorpion stabbed the frog. Knox fired, and the back of the kid's head burst into flames. He knew right away that he might be fucked. Eddie came running down the pier.

"Jesus, Deke! What the fuck is wrong with you?"

"I stopped a drug dealer who was running from me."

"Yeah." Eddie looked down at the kid. His head was smoldering, sending a burnt-hair smell up. He was a cool surf cowboy, now he's mash on the sand. "That was really crazy, Deke."

"I know. I'm sorry. I won't do it again."

Eddie glanced around the beach. Luckily the kid had made it to the wooden piers, and relatively out of sight. "Look; we can cover this. Just this once we can cover this. But you can't go under the bridge again. They run, let 'em go. I can't have a partner who kills everything he sees. What is it? Do you Want to kill people?"

"I won't do it again," Knox said. "How do we handle this?"

"We blame it on the Manx. We blame everything on the Manx. Just this time. But this can't happen again. We're making good buck down here, Deke. You know what you're doing and I know what I'm doing. But you gotta get out from under the bridge. These rich kids run away from you it's because they know you won't chase them. They don't have the three gee ticket, they sprint on you and you come back on them another time. This kid the Manx killed, he's got parents, and the parents probably got money. I'll cover you this time—I know how to do it. But just this once. You turn into a crazy skink-killer, it's on you. Be smart, or be stupid, it's your call."

"I got you."

Eddie looked down at the blonde kid, his skull blasted apart. "Shit. Let's get out of here."

Nine . . .

"It won't be long, Sis—it won't be long and I'll have the money to get us out of here."

"I told you; I don't want to get out of here."

"Lizzie, this city is going to go up in flames. It's going mad. Things are going to get really bad here really fast."

"Things are going to get really bad everywhere. You think money is going to cure that? It's no better out there than it is in here. There is only one place to escape to."

"No. You're giving up on life—that's all you're doing."

"Maybe. So what?"

"What that is—Dream; it's putting yourself in a coma and then you die. That's all it is. Your perfect story; your perfect dream, it's all mental bullshit. It's a god damn drug, Lizzie!"

"You know, it's ironic, Deke. You've been hooked on Dream most of your life. It defined your very life. Only you never realized it."

"I worked to make a living. I never had the luxury of going into Dreality."

"And now all you can think about is her. You can preach and lecture all you want. But you think about her. One day nothing else will matter."

"We've got to try. We can't all just prop ourselves against a building and die."

"If you die here in this madness or you die at the end of your story—everything has to die. It's whether you want to die under a bridge or whether you want to die in your story."

Knox stared down at his hands. They were not the skillful hands that had shot the arrows true. These were hands blue with veins, tired from the years of living. Hands that had murdered people under bridges and in alleys. Old rotten hands that couldn't keep wives and couldn't save those he had promised to save. I can't save myself, he thought.

"When you take Dream, where you go, it's peaceful, right?"

"Yes, it is."

"Where I go there's war. It's very beautiful; it's magical. But there's war and violence. Why does that have to keep hounding me? Doc Grey told me that Dream just takes you to where you want to be. But I don't want war and violence. I've had enough of that; now I just want peace. But my story ain't giving me that. I'm done with it, and I won't go back. There are enough evil creatures to fight here; I don't need an army of them storming the gates."

Liz smiled. "Storming the gates?"

Knox looked at the window in his apartment. "The guy you have out there. True love at last?"

"Yes. True love."

"And when you go out there forever, and they're scraping your body off the pavement and sending it to the ovens . . ."

"I'll die in the arms of my only true love."

"That's a pretty speech. Doc Grey would approve. He's all in favor of mass suicide, cleaning the humans out of the world. As long as it's not him."

"Have you ever wondered if he's right?"

"No. What about his beliefs is right?"

"That people have tipped the balance, and that this is finally the Judgment."

"I know you're into religion, Sis; that's fine. I think the Bible is against suicide. Against purposely destroying the body that God made for you."

"You're trying to save me, Big Brother, from my destiny. I love you, and I will always love you. We were unlucky enough to live in the dying world. I hope you find happiness out there. Let me go where I need to go."

"Liz—"

"No, shut up. Let me go. I know where I have to go. There are too many humans crawling across this world. It's that simple. I believe God sent us Dream in order to clean the world of humans. His way of taking us to heaven and ridding the earth of our bodies. Dr. Grey is right: there are too many of us. The world is cleansing itself of human beings, in order to survive."

"That's what I'm talking about, Sis; to survive."

"Some don't want to survive. I don't want to survive."

"Jesus God—"

"Go. Escape. Find something out there. Get away from this, if you can. You could never have saved me; you could never have saved yourself."

"I tried," he said.

"Yes, you did. You tried with Johnny and now you're trying with me. You tried with yourself."

He let out a sigh. "Things are going to get bad here. Everything's falling apart fast. They're loading up dream-deads by the hundreds. There's these people—the Manx. You see an upside down black cross on some guy's arm, you stay away from him. Okay?"

"Okay," she said.

"Every cop I know is putting away cash to get out. We know what's coming. Lizzie, I've stashed a lot of cash. If I give you money, are you going to use it for food and rent, or are you going to blow it on Dream?"

"You wouldn't ask if you didn't know."

"Jesus . . . Look, I'm out there making the best money I ever made. I'm with a partner, and we're working good and shooting nobody. This is my chance to get out of here."

"You'll never get out of here. The only way to get out is to go into your story, and stay there until you die."

"Escape with drugs. That's the coward's way. That's not living, it's dying on a street corner, and then you're ashes dumped in a landfill."

"Or dead under a bridge."

"Sis—I don't know what to tell you. I promised to take care of you. I promised that you'd never go the way Johnny went—"

"You think about her, don't you?" Liz smiled at him. "You can't stop thinking about her, and how you might save her."

Ten . . .

"So I'm officially retired," Doc Grey said, pouring a vodka and adding a dap of orange juice. "It's the great kill and the great clean-up. Things fall apart, the center cannot hold, that kind of thing. I hope you like orange juice with your vodka, Derek."

Knox took the vodka. "Yes," he said. "How's retirement?"

"Boring. Here at the end of the world it's strangely boring."

"Be grateful," Knox said.

"Oh, I am. My life was more than I ever deserved. And now I plan to go completely into my Dream story until it's over. You might find that a bit fatalistic."

"You're going to give up like everybody else."

Dr. Grey studied him with tense eyes: "There's no giving up. We almost destroyed this world with our arrogance and greed and evil that we never realized was evil. This world does not deserve to be raped and pillaged by creatures like us. It's that simple."

"So we all commit suicide, we all die and rid the world of us."

"Too many humans are here destroying the planet," Doc Grey said. "It's that simple. The only hope for this planet to go on living is if human beings are gone. I've lived beyond my time; now I'll rid the earth of me, and hope it heals itself in some small way."

"They say Dream's the best way to commit suicide."

"I'm sure it is." Doc Grey smiled at him. "I see in your eyes that you've taken Dream."

"Twice," Knox admitted.

"Dream is God. It's God giving us a passage to Heaven; it's God ridding the world of our stinking, raping bodies. Our sin, our evil. Dream takes you where you were always meant to go. I hope you find the way, Derek."

Eleven . . .

HE RODE WITH CASSIEL THROUGH Summerwood forest, a company of soldiers flanking them. In real life Knox had never been on a horse; but like the miracle of the bow and arrows, he had an inexplicable skill, as if he had been born in the saddle. It gave him hope that he might have other unknown powers, maybe even to gain control of this story.

He followed Cassiel around the narrow trail that dropped down to a simple wooden bridge spanning the silver forest stream. The skies were growing overcast, and soon a light mist floated down through the trees. Oak and maple trees towered over them. The primal scent of nature overwhelmed him.

I created this world, he thought. I willed that Cassiel fall in love with me, and she is in love with me. I made these flowers grow along this silver stream. I can save this; I can save everything.

"When we climb out of this glade," Cassiel said darkly, breaking the misty spell. "We will see the armies of the Garmen."

The mounted soldiers would glance at her, their princess, wondering how this stranger had enchanted her. They still believe I'm a wizard, Knox thought. Let's hope I am.

"I created all of this," he murmured to himself. "I've given myself powers. How to control the story?"

"Why do you keep saying things like that, My Love?" Cassiel was studying him.

He smiled at her. She wore her riding outfit, the forest green dress fringed with white and grey fur. Her long auburn hair fell below a jacket hood of silver wolf.

"Like what?"

"That you have created all of this. That this is not real."

"I'm sorry. But it's strange: I've given myself powers that I never had. I've given myself skills with weapons and horse riding. But somehow I don't seem in control of this."

"You always speak so strangely. How can anyone—even a wizard—control the world?"

"I don't want to see this world destroyed. I've already seen one world destroyed."

They rode out of the forest to sunlight and a tall hill. In the distant east was a smudgy horizon that spoke of fire and smoke. They couldn't actually see the faraway armies of the enemy, but Knox had no doubt that they were there. He did see people snaking down the road that led eastward; peasant families desperately fleeing toward Summerwood Castle.

"They are only a few days away," Cassiel said.

"Like the Manx."

Twelve . . .

"YOU GOT A RED FLAG, Deke." Hugo frowned at him.

"A red—what!"

"The last guy you put away in Self Defense—Blondie?"

"I didn't pop anybody. I heard it was the Manx that got that guy."

"He was Manx, you fool."

Knox took a deep breath. "So what?'

"So everything. Jesus, are you going crazy?"

"It's all about popping the Skinks when they try to kill you; then scoop up the bounty. Who's really stupid here, Hugo?"

"You are!"

"That's the way it's been out there since Dream. You know that. What should I have done—Really arrested him?"

Hugo was staring at him in·a way that made Knox feel like a lunatic, and it pissed him off, and it scared him.

"The war's over," Hugo said. "We lost it; we didn't stand a chance. You think you got smarts, but you're clueless. The Manx have been working for P.D. since the last time you got laid, and dinosaurs were running around."

"I kind of figured that."

"No, you didn't."

"And I didn't know he was a Manx! Hell, he was carrying a Stabber—top of the line."

"You got lucky." Hugo looked out the dusty window. "Or not."

"Hey, I'm not going through that red flag shit! And fuck him, if he was a Manx or not. I do my job. I bust Dream dealers, and if they pull a pipe on me, I make them see black, as quick as I can. You must remember how it was, Hugo. Your fat butt sitting at a desk can't forget how it is out there. A Skink pulls on me, what else can I do?"

"Don't pop another one."

Knox started to speak, then got smart. "I won't," he said. He stared at the window. A departmental red flag was bad enough; he didn't need the Manx after him. "What is this, Hugo? What am I supposed to do?"

"Get the fuck out, buddy."

Knox felt the worms crawling in his stomach. "I'm a Lieutenant Police Officer for the city of New York! I do the god damned job I'm paid to do."

"Shit; are you that stupid now? You want a Manx putting you black in some alley or under some bridge? You know that's gonna happen."

Knox looked around Hugo's office. "How many cameras are on us—buddy? How many cameras are listening to us?"

"Enough," Hugo said. "You got red-flagged, Lieutenant. And I have to place you on suspension."

"For what!"

"Enough! Don't you know what I'm saying? You're lucky they're giving you a chance; for your long record of service."

"A chance for what?"

"To get out—to escape. Before you get splashed."

Thirteen . . .

"Okay, I'm going to try and escape." They were at Dr. Grey's house, a comfortable ranch just off 73rd and Wishful. They had a last whiskey.

"I hope you do. I've found my escape, and you know what it is; what it's always been. I spent most of my life keeping people alive and campaigning to kill them. I've lived a life of irony, if nothing else."

"I suppose it's no secret that I've killed people."

"No secret at all."

"People I didn't know. People who didn't really mean me any harm. I know that I deserve to die for the decisions I've made, the things I've done."

"Maybe we all deserve to die. I don't make a complicated thing of this, what's happening to this world. There just got to be too many of us, that's all. A scale was tipped; maybe by the birth of the last fatal human child. And then the Earth had had enough."

"That sounds cold," Knox said.

"If you look at the earth as a living thing that has to protect herself from destruction, it shouldn't be surprising. Damn near everything that ever lived on Earth went extinct. Maybe every one of them thought they were special. When you cure yourself of infection, you're destroying a world of billions—and you don't think twice about it. If something infects you and threatens to destroy you—"

"Hey, Dream wasn't made by nature—it was made by Gustav Arnold."

Grey seemed very tired. He didn't want to argue. "Maybe you're right, I don't know."

"I'm going to try and escape. All I need is a little more time and a little more money."

Grey sipped his whiskey. "Things are better when you're drunk—and you know that time is running out. I've got my own escape strategy. Maybe you'll get yours."

"I'm trying to get Liz to go with me. At least we can get out of the city."

"I think Liz wants to go where I'm going."

"Don't say that. It's cowardly. It's giving up. It's suicide."

"Is it?" Grey stared off. "I don't know."

"I do. It's a drug, nothing more. You can't just take a drug and go off into another world and just die there."

"Yes, you can. How many millions have?"

"There's got to be a better way out. One day soon I'm just going to go—get out of the city. Go out there to the countryside; find a small town where people aren't going insane."

"I'm afraid you'll find that they're going insane everywhere."

Fourteen . . .

THE NEXT NIGHT EDDIE FRIED a kid right under the Pallisades pier.

Knox couldn't believe his eyes. He ran down and stepped through the pilings. The ocean made a smelly dead fish air down here. You had to walk sloppy, over moss and slush. Eddie was cleaning the kid of his money and drugs. There was a focused madness in Eddie's eyes. It was dark down here, thanks for that.

"What the fuck are you doing? Jesus—what!" Knox stared down at the kid, his head splashed in the dirty sand. "I can't believe this!" Knox glanced around for witnesses. "You said—"

"Shut up. I don't think anybody saw me do it, and it don't matter anymore. Everything's changed."

"What are you talking about?"

"I'm getting my ass laid off in two weeks. DEA's getting rid of guys they know went off the farm. I've been off the farm a long time, and so have you. Once we're no longer the law, we're dead in a ditch."

"Jesus. So you start blowing away skinks?"

"Time's running out fast, Partner. You're next to go—you can't be that stupid. The Manx got a fucking hit on you, and the Manx are all over P.D. Listen: We both have to scoop up every dime and every pill we can as fast as we can. The skinks give us all their cash and all their Dream and we don't pop 'em. Otherwise—figure it out."

"How fast is this going on?"

"Like two days fast. From now I'm making my break. I'm going to scoop up as much cash and Dream as I can, then I'm gone. Remember: out there Dream's gonna be more valuable than money."

"You want me to help you just kill the skinks and rip them off?"

"You been doing that all along, Partner; ever since Dream came along."

"Two days."

"Then I'm out of here. Word at your P.D.; you don't have two days. Get together just what you might need, Partner, and escape. Get out on side streets, that's how I'm gonna do it. The Manx might be watching the main freeways."

Knox fingered the red pills in his pocket. "Two days," he said.

"Regular people that don't bother the Manx, they'll go on living until it really falls down around them. Cops like us, we don't stand a chance unless we get the fuck out fast. You think you still got a job, a skink-killer like you? I promise you—you ain't got a job. And the worms are eating your guts alive."

"Yeah." Knox looked down at the dead kid. "I don't think I can do this anymore."

"Okay. Here's half the kid's stash." Eddie handed it over. "Plenty of reds here—but sell 'em, don't do 'em."

"Maybe there's nothing else." Knox looked down at the kid-corpse in the sand.

"Well, I'm going super-hunting for the next two days; you're welcome to join me."

"No. I think I'm done."

"Don't take those reds."

Eddie left him there in Pallisades, never to be seen again. Knox climbed up to his car and drove off. When he had turned the key, he half-expected it to blow up.

It was four o'clock in the afternoon. He was scared—he was scared. Night would be here soon, and that would have to be it. He had planned and stashed, but you never really are ready for escape.

Fifteen . . .

THE DOOR TO THE COFFEE shop played a cartoon melody as he stepped inside. Liz took a 15 minute break and sat with him over coffee. She munched on a granola biscuit, he wasn't hungry.

"You've been going back there, Big Brother." She gave him one of her ironic half-smiles. "I see it in your eyes."

"That doesn't matter. I'm getting out tonight, Sis."

She stared at him. "Tonight? You're going to walk away from your career, your apartment, your car—tonight?"

"Yes. I'm going to try and hoof it out of here; that's the safest way. I can be out of the city in four days."

"I don't—I don't know what to say. Are you . . . okay?"

"I'll go to my apartment this evening to get everything I can carry that matters. Then I walk away."

"Just walk away . . . isn't this a little sudden?"

"You know I've been planning this, Lizzie. Only now I don't want you coming with me, because there are scary guys out there who want to kill me. I'll be risking my life just going back to my place—but I have to take that chance."

"Derek, this is . . . I've lost three good friends this month! Now you?"

"You lost them to Dream, didn't you? They went dream-dead."

"We call it going to the other side."

"Yeah. Well, I wanted to give you a hug, Sis, and say goodbye. I can't stick around long." He glanced out the coffee shop window at the street. "It might be dangerous, I'm not sure."

"God, Deke!" She hugged him and cried against him. "I don't know how it got so . . ."

"I don't think anyone does. I love you, Sis."

Sixteen . . .

ALLISON HAD GIVEN HIM HER gate code, and he waited
for the aluminum gate to whine open, allowing his police
car inside.

This was Cedar Park, and even the gardeners glared
at his car. Rent-a-cops scooted around everywhere, as
if the wolves weren't coming to chew their throats. One
of them pulled him over (a joke?), and Knox tapped his
palm and showed his badge.

Dream was here, Allison had assured him. Dream
was very discretely distributed here in this lovely gated
community. Discretely distributed everywhere.

She welcomed him into the splendor of her home,
her life. It was a spacious apartment of oriental design;
only a few pieces, precious and expensive, adorning the
space. He liked it.

He thought of Cassiel.

"Ally—are you making plans to get out?"

She looked at him. "Get out where?"

"Away!"

"Derek, you are paranoid."

"No, I'm not. I won't stay long. I have to leave right now. I only wanted to see you again and to tell you!"

"Tell me what?"

"Get out, Ally—before it's too late."

"Derek, I know it's getting bad. Times are—"

"You don't know, Ally. You don't know!"

"Know what?"

"How bad it's going to get. It's going to hit fast, and it's going to be bad."

"Derek . . . calm down."

He gave her a hug and smiled at her. "I hope you're one of the ones who make it," he said.

Seventeen . . .

HE HID OUT THE REST of the evening under the Newton Railroad Bridge, a shadow squatting on the abutment. Every hour or so he emerged to study his apartment complex, just two blocks down the street.

The Manx weren't sophisticated; they didn't have to be. Maybe they'd be content to just scare him away.

Away where?

He gazed at the orange sun as it crawled to dusk. The stone skyscrapers of the city darkened into a silhouette of dark still. How fast things can fall apart and leave you lost. A police officer—a troll squatting under a bridge. It was a dream, getting out of this; it was a dream escaping to some countryside. It was something he always wanted—but it was nothing more than a dream. To save his brother and sister from this? It was a dream.

When the sun went down, he crept up to his apartment, unlocked the door and went in with a flashlight. He'd practiced this. He went back and got his stash out of the wall, hefted the backpack, and walked quickly down the dark street, leaving everything else behind. Escape was possible. But he suddenly didn't want escape. A weary truth fell over him suddenly, like a dark but comforting blanket. He had never been destined to escape.

He walked up Newton Street to 7th. He had a couple changes of clothes; plenty of cash and plenty of Dream. Every worm in his belly rolled. The city around him was strangely quiet this night. Fewer people every day. The city—no money left—was having a hard time disposing of the dead. He would still have the gut-worms, even out there in the world beyond the city.

He sat and rested on a gluey bench. The city stank around him; but he didn't want to move. The night air was dull and sultry. Grease, oil-smell, garbage—death. There were different kinds of dreams. It was a dream, him escaping somewhere out there, after what he'd done. It was a dream him saving Johnny and Liz. Suddenly he felt very tired. Maybe God was calling him home. Maybe not.

He took four red pills out of his knapsack. The sack that was supposed to get him out of the city—out there. He looked at the pills. He hoped Allison would get out. He hoped Lizzie would find a way to escape. Old Grey wouldn't get out—he never wanted to.

Hell, he even wanted Eddie to escape.

The night air was dull and sultry. He looked at the pills in his palm. Red tablets, nothing more. Four reds would definitely put him out of this for good. Forever. And be Dream-dead and put out of your coma and go off to the ovens.

Forever is a long time out there. It's not what Allison or Liz said about it—or Dr. Grey or Hugo. It is the very idea of what is real.

Eighteen . . .

"DEREKNOX!" SHE CRIED. "YOU'RE AWAKE."

"Cassiel."

"When you sleep it is as if you are dead."

"I don't think I'll be sleeping much anymore."

He got up from a green woolen bed. He looked around him. The air smelled slightly smoky. Summerwood castle let stabs of bright sun in. "It stopped raining."

"Yes." She gave him a soft and mournful smile. "We have little time, My Love."

"I know. I thought I could change this. But I can't."

"The Garmen are at the gates."

"I know." He could hear them out there, a heathen roar. It was a distant roar, like far off ocean waves. He wondered if his whole life had brought him inevitably to this dream. He had maybe always lived in his mind—or worse, the past—and had only operated in reality for duty and survival. No matter now. This was as real as anything he had ever felt.

He rolled off the bed and hugged Cassiel. He kissed her. He felt the world against him, melting into him. He knew that out there, in New York City, this was the end of him. It was only the collectors finding him and ending him. But now he was joyfully alive.

"At first I thought I could control this story," he said. "If I could have, I would at least have tried to escape with you."

"I would never have left Summerwood."

"I know."

"There was never enough time for us, My Love." She cried against him. "I do not know who you are, or what you are. I only know that I fell in love with you the moment I saw you—I do not know why. At a time of despair and sorrow you came to me and made me feel hope—and love."

Knox listened to the roar out there, getting louder. "I think, My Love, that now we need to go out there and fight."

They went quickly out to the battlements, Cassiel saying, "My father says they will breech the west wall. We cannot stop them."

"Then I'd better get to the west wall."

"I am with you, Dereknox."

They ran up the battlement, brushing past frantic soldiers in scarlet and black. The west wall of the casle was teetering; the earth shuddered as giant boulders arched across the sky and slammed home. Summerwood soldiers had assembled to meet the enemy when the storm came. King Xerros stood at their front, a wobbly old warrior staring calmly at death. Knox began shooting arrows over the wall, felling Garmen warriors who gathered for their charge.

Soon enough the wall fell, and Garmen came spilling into the green-park of Summerwood castle. A violent mass of fighters fell at one another like mad animals, and Cassiel cried out as her father fell to a barbarian club. Knox fired into the horde of Garmen until he was out of arrows. His heart hammered his chest; he had never felt so alive. This was where his life and his dream had taken him. He only wished he had had more time with Cassiel.

It could be that he had created the Garmen in the model of the Manx, a nightmare force creeping over his life. Below the battlement the soldiers of Summerwood were overwhelmed; they lay scattered in the green swards and rock pools. Smoke rose over the countryside, fouling the rain-sweet air.

He held Cassiel as they stared down at the end. The barbarians in hides and furs poured in through the west wall and began swarming up the battlements. It was time to die. He felt no fear; only a bittersweet sadness that he had not had more time.

"I thought I could control this story," he whispered into her ear. "I thought I might be able to save this."

"You stayed when you could have run away," she said. "Now, die with me, My Love."

She drew her sword; Knox drew his.

Everything is a story, monumental or not. Every little life, dead in bed or scraped off the pavement is a story enveloped in dreams. Everyone knows how stories end . . .

The dawn cleanup crew pulled over to the bus bench at 7th and Newton, and two men in the white outfits got out of the white truck. They examined Derek Knox to ensure that he was dream-dead. Finally one of the men pulled out a spring syringe and jabbed him in the neck, finishing the job.

"Hey, check this out." The haz-mat guy pressed Knox's dead palm and they looked at the badge that appeared on his wrist. "This guy was P.D. Detective, narcotics squad."

"Not anymore."

The men quickly bagged up Knox's body and loaded it into the white truck.

"He looked happy enough," one of them said.

"Don't they all."

THE END.